BBC Children's Books
Published by the Penguin Group
Penguin Books Ltd, 80 Strand, London, WC2R ORL, England
Penguin Group (USA) Inc., 375 Hudson Street, New York 10014, USA
Penguin Books (Australia) Ltd, 707 Collins Street, Melbourne,
Victoria 3008, Australia
(A division of Pearson Australia Group PTY Ltd)
Penguin Group (NZ), 67 Apollo Drive, Rosedale, Auckland
0632, New Zealand (a division of Pearson New Zealand Ltd)
Canada, India, South Africa
Published by BBC Children's Books, 2013
Text and design © Children's Character Books
Written by Moray Laing
Comic illustrations by John Ross
Comic colours by James Offredi
Pages 38-39 illustrated by Lee Sullivan
001

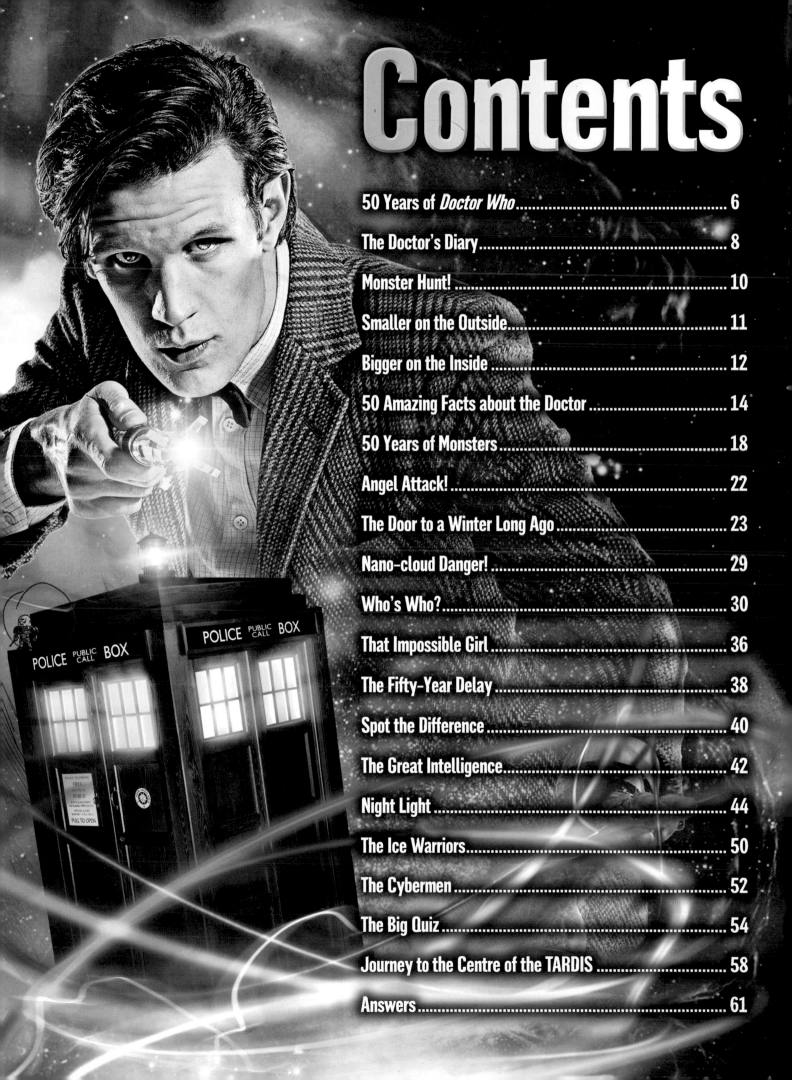

Contents

50 Years of
DOCTOR WHO

TIME FLIES WHEN YOU'RE A TIME LORD!

In the Beginning

On 23 November 1963, *Doctor Who* appeared on television for the very first time. The BBC wanted a new science fiction series for Saturday evenings and the result was a programme about a mysterious old man who could travel in time as well as space. He was known as the Doctor, but nobody really knew who he was. **Doctor who?**

An Unearthly Child

The first-ever episode was all about a girl called Susan Foreman. When two of her schoolteachers discover that Susan lives in a police box in a junkyard, her grandfather – a grumpy old man called the Doctor – feels threatened at being found out and decides to whisk them away into time and space...

The Doctor didn't have as much control over the TARDIS as he does now — so this meant the teachers thought they might never get home. And that's how it all began — exciting adventures in the past, the present and in the future, on alien planets and so many amazing worlds.

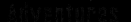

But who is the Doctor?

Even after fifty years, there's still a big question mark over who the Doctor actually is. We do know he's a Time Lord who has met famous people from history and creatures from nightmares. He's also one of the bravest and cleverest men you are ever likely to meet — and he never walks away from danger.

Happy Anniversary!

By the end of 2013, there will have been 240 stories, made up of nearly 800 individual episodes of *Doctor Who*. The Doctor has regenerated ten times, meaning he's had eleven different bodies and has travelled in the TARDIS with nearly fifty companions. And fifty years of saving the universe and travelling in time and space is definitely worth celebrating.

HAPPY ANNIVERSARY, DOCTOR WHO.
HERE'S TO MANY, MANY MORE ADVENTURES!

THE DOCTOR'S DIARY

HELPING THE DALEKS

There I was about to enjoy a cup of tea and a scone when suddenly a strange figure sent me a dream message. Psychic projection, massively clever. It wanted me to head to the old home of the Daleks - the planet Skaro - a place I never wanted to return to. Well, of course, it was a trap... and the Daleks wanted my help for a change, which was different.

DINOSAURS ON A SPACESHIP!

I love dinosaurs (who doesn't?) so I couldn't believe my eyes when I arrived on a space ark the size of Canada. Blimey! It was full of them! I thought I'd need a gang to explore that ark, so took my old friend Queen Neffy, a hunter called Riddell and my extremely good chums, the Ponds. Sort of materialised the TARDIS around Rory's Dad, too. Must be more careful in future.

LOSING THE PONDS

Dear, brave Ponds. I've been travelling with them for so long now. But today it ended. The Weeping Angels... New York... River... I can hardly bring myself to write it all down - it's too painful. But I know that they're OK, happy and together, as they should be. I never learn. It's dangerous travelling with me.

I SHOULD PROBABLY TRAVEL ALONE.

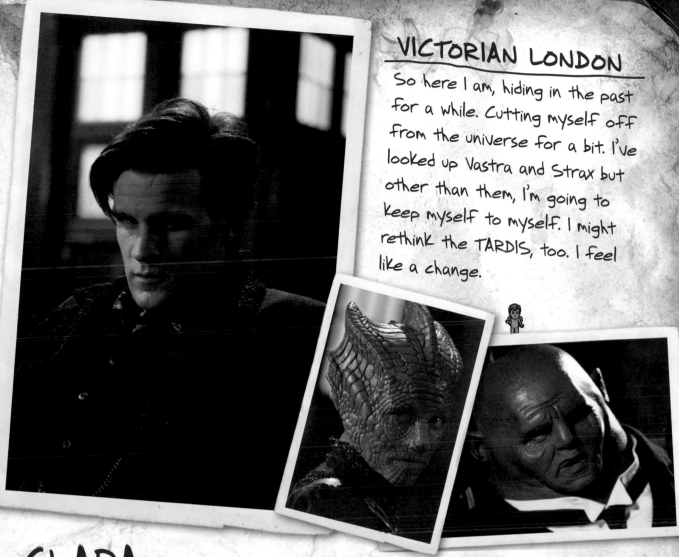

VICTORIAN LONDON

So here I am, hiding in the past for a while. Cutting myself off from the universe for a bit. I've looked up Vastra and Strax but other than them, I'm going to keep myself to myself. I might rethink the TARDIS, too. I feel like a change.

CLARA

Nothing makes sense about Clara. Absolutely nothing. I don't know who she is and I don't understand her. Maybe I should just ask her? I've met her three times - and the same woman has died twice. She's now going to travel with me and somebody has just told me I have to trust her. Is this another trap?

I'LL WORK IT OUT. ONE DAY...

MONSTER HUNT!

THERE ARE FIFTY HORRORS HIDING THROUGHOUT THIS BOOK AND THEY ARE ALL TRYING TO ESCAPE! HELP THE DOCTOR TRACK THEM DOWN BEFORE THEY SUCCEED.

When you find each creature, put a tick next to the image below.

You can find out about all these creatures on page eighteen!

Smaller on the Outside

The Doctor's TARDIS is the most incredible machine!

The light flashes when the TARDIS appears and disappears. The bulb needs changing now and again.

St John Ambulance sign.

Message to public and police. Conceals a telephone.

The lock opens with an ordinary Yale key (or a click of the Doctor's fingers!).

POLICE PUBLIC CALL BOX

POLICE PUBLIC CALL BOX

POLICE TELEPHONE
FREE
FOR USE OF
PUBLIC
ADVICE & ASSISTANCE
OBTAINABLE IMMEDIATELY
OFFICERS & CARS
RESPOND TO ALL CALLS
PULL TO OPEN

Appearance

The outside of the TARDIS is a battered old blue police box. The TARDIS should be able to change its appearance wherever it goes. However, after the Doctor landed in London in the 1960s the chameleon circuit broke and it became stuck as a police box. The Doctor could fix it, but he likes the way it looks!

Boxes like this were once found on streets in England and Scotland from the late 1920s up until the early 1970s. The public and police could use them to get help if they'd seen a crime or an accident. The light on top would attract the attention of a police officer or a passing police car.

BIGGER ON THE INSIDE

Stepping through the doors of the police box can shock most people – it's safe to say that nothing prepares you for what's inside!

What is a TARDIS?

Grown on the planet Gallifrey, a TARDIS is one of the most powerful ships in the universe. The name TARDIS stands for Time And Relative Dimension In Space, and it can go anywhere and to any time in the universe.

POLICE PUBLIC CALL BOX

Did you know?

Without the TARDIS the Doctor says he's nothing – just a spaceman on a rock.

The console room

The first room you enter is the console room. It contains the main controls and is also the safest room in the whole ship. If necessary, the TARDIS can create several copies of the console room to keep its occupants safe.

Power

The Eye of Harmony is the power source of the TARDIS. It's an exploding star about to become a black hole. Time Lords discovered how to take the star from its orbit and suspend it in a permanent state of decay inside a spaceship.

Engine

The engine is the heart of the TARDIS and is found deep inside the ship. It can be quite tricky to get to it – especially if the TARDIS is trying to scare you away from it!

Last of its kind

After the Last Great Time War, there was only one TARDIS left in the universe – and that's the one you are looking at – the Doctor's. It may be unpredictable, and it might go wrong sometimes, but it always takes him to where it thinks he needs to go.

Archived rooms

Rooms in the TARDIS can be deleted or remodelled. The Doctor has changed the appearance of the inside several times so far. To keep things neat, the TARDIS archives them. The one thing that remains constant is a six-sided console in the centre of the room. Here are a few of the earlier designs.

Gleaming white interior

Wood-panelled

High-tech design

Organic and glowing green

Bright and bold

13

50 AMAZING Facts About the Doctor!

THERE IS NO ONE QUITE LIKE THE DOCTOR. HERE ARE SOME OF THE BEST FACTS ABOUT THIS INCREDIBLE TIME LORD!

1 He has only recently realised how much he likes hearing people say 'Doctor who?'

2 Hardly anyone knows the Doctor's proper name.

3 He calls himself the Doctor, but has never revealed why!

4 Theta Sigma was his nickname when he was younger.

5 He's over a thousand years old.

6 He ran away from his home planet, Gallifrey. It was a beautiful place with twin suns, snowy mountains and red grass.

7 When Gallifrey was destroyed, the Doctor became the last of the Time Lords.

8 In truth, the Doctor stole the TARDIS, although he prefers to say he borrowed it.

9 The Daleks called the Doctor 'The Oncoming Storm' and also 'The Predator'.

10 But, thanks to Oswin Oswald, the Daleks no longer know who the Doctor is...

11 He has two hearts.

12 He tries never to take the TARDIS into battle because it's now the most powerful ship in the universe.

13 He once took a bike from Henry the Ninth, while Henry was trapped under a piano.

14 When he was exiled on Earth, he had an old yellow car called Bessie!

15 He can read books in seconds...

16 ...and he's also mentioned in a lot of books.

17 He was a Dad, once.

18 He had a granddaughter called Susan.

19 He never just walks away from difficult situations, he stays to sort things out.

20 He thinks the Lake District is lovely – they do a nice scone in 1927, apparently.

21 He has seen the birth of the universe...

22 ...and he's also seen the end.

23 He knows secrets that must never be spoken.

24 The Doctor can't always control the TARDIS.

25 He used to travel with a robot dog called K-9. He has built three other models of the same dog, two of which he gave to Sarah Jane Smith.

POLICE PUBLIC CALL BOX

POLICE PUBLIC CALL BOX

26 He likes the word 'toggle'. He thinks it's a nice word and excellent verb.

27 He likes to shout 'Geronimo!' before doing something dangerous!

28 The Doctor is allergic to certain gasses that can turn celery purple, so he used to wear a stick of celery on his jacket.

29 He can put himself into a coma, if he needs to.

30 He went to an academy on Gallifrey.

31 He is qualified as a medical doctor – he took a degree in nineteenth century Glasgow.

32 He's also got a degree in making cheese!

33 He was given an honorary degree from Cambridge in 1960.

34 The Time Lords once wiped his memory of how to use the TARDIS.

35 He used to live in a house halfway up a mountain on Gallifrey.

36 Like all Time Lords, he was taken away from his family when he was just eight years old and made to look into the Untempered Schism.

37 When he was younger, he liked to run in the fields that led to Mount Perdition all day with the Master. They were good friends.

38 Shortly after regenerating, the Tenth Doctor had his hand cut off by a Sycorax. Captain Jack Harkness later found it.

39 Luckily, in the first fifteen hours after a regeneration, he can use cellular energy to repair any damaged limbs – so he grew back his hand!

40 He has a different metabolism to humans – so don't give him Earth medicine, as it could kill him.

41 He is married to River Song – but they have the strangest life together! Both are time travellers, so their pasts and futures are all jumbled up.

42 He's met so many famous figures from history – including Queen Nefertiti, Charles Dickens, William Shakespeare, Agatha Christie and Winston Churchill. Many are good friends.

43 He once got engaged to Marilyn Monroe.

44 He belongs to Virginia Woolf's bowling team.

45 He's telepathic and can look inside people's minds by touching their heads.

46 The Eleventh Doctor is an accomplished footballer.

47 While exiled on Earth he went by the name of Dr John Smith.

48 When he regenerates, his accent can change quite dramatically.

49 Although it's very dangerous, he has met his other earlier selves on several occasions!

50 HE'S BRILLIANT AT PRACTICALLY EVERYTHING!

50 YEARS OF MONSTERS!

THE DOCTOR HAS MADE LOTS OF ENEMIES OVER THE LAST FIFTY YEARS AND HERE ARE FIFTY OF THE SCARIEST!

1 DALEK

Probably the most dangerous race in the whole universe. If you're not a Dalek and they don't need you, they will exterminate you.

2 CYBERMEN

Tall, silver men with no emotions. Their ultimate goal is to convert everyone to be like them.

3 WEEPING ANGEL

Scary stone creatures that can only move if no one is looking. Blink and they'll get you.

4 EMPTY CHILD

If this 'child' touches you, you'll immediately turn into a gas mask zombie, too.

5 THE BEAST

Imprisoned on the planet of Krop Tor, this massive fire-breathing creature is best avoided.

6 AUTON

A plastic dummy powered by the Nestene. Beware of their drop-down 'hand' guns.

7 CLOCKWORK ROBOT

Elegant robots that thought a human brain could repair their spaceship.

8 KRILLITANE

Shape-shifting bat creatures that once took over a London school.

9 SLITHEEN

Family of criminals from the planet Raxacoricofallapatorius.

10 SYCORAX

Bone-headed warrior race that tried to enslave the human race one Christmas.

11 WEREWOLF

This creature once bit Queen Victoria in Scotland 1879. Ouch.

12 THE EMPRESS OF THE RACNOSS

Huge spider creature that wanted to wake her hibernating children.

13 CARRIONITES

Cackling witch-faced hags that use words to channel energy.

14 DALEK SEC HYBRID

A human Dalek – the result of an experiment to revive the Dalek race.

15 TOCLAFANE

This is what humans become trillions of years in the future.

16 HEAVENLY HOST

Robotic menaces found on-board the spaceliner *Titanic*.

17 ADIPOSE

Sweet little monsters made from fat. Yuck!

18 PYROVILES

Fierce rock creatures that crashed to Earth.

19 OOD

Aliens used as slaves in the forty-second century. Dangerous when their eyes glow red.

20 VESPIFORM

Shape-shifting insect race resembling giant wasps in their natural form.

21 VASHTA NERADA

Flesh-eating creatures – the name means 'the shadows that melt the flesh'. Avoid.

22 TIME BEETLE

Large insect creature that can change time. Don't let it get on your back.

23 JUDOON

Hulking rhino-like race used as police by the Shadow Proclamation and others.

24 GANGER

Clone creatures created from a gooey substance called the Flesh.

25 SCARECROW

Lumbering army brought to life by the Family of Blood.

26 SILENCE

Nightmare race that can edit themselves out of your memories. And in a word – terrifying!

29 SILURIANS
Reptile humanoids that hibernated under the Earth millions of years ago.

27 DALEK SKELETON
Horrific result of Dalek Nano-cloud meeting dead humans.

28 SONTARANS
Advanced warrior race of clones that like war and fighting.

30 HEADLESS MONKS
Warrior race. You must never lower their hoods.

31 PEG DOLL
Sinister dolls. Their touch can transform you into one of them. So don't touch!

32 CYBERMATS
Cybernetic creations of the Cybermen. Look quite sweet, but they'll kill you.

33 MINOTAUR
Multi-horned creature that insists on being worshipped. Praise him.

34 GUNSLINGER
Cyborg that now protects a town called Mercy.

35 THE SHAKRI
Pest controllers of the universe.

37 SNOWMEN
Nightmare snowmen created by the Great Intelligence.

36 CHERUB
Smaller versions of Weeping Angels, and just as deadly.

38 ICE GOVERNESS
Also created by the Great Intelligence. Ice-fanged and deadly.

39 ICE WARRIORS
Deadly warriors from the planet Mars.

40 TIME ZOMBIES
Horrific future versions of the Doctor and Clara in the TARDIS.

41 SEA DEVIL
Cousins of the Silurians from under the sea.

42 VOC ROBOTS
Robot servants on a sandminer that were reprogrammed to kill.

43 YETI
Large robotic puppets for the Great Intelligence.

44 RASTON WARRIOR ROBOT
Super-fast robot, and the most perfect killing machine ever invented.

45 HAEMOVORE
Vampire-like servants of an ancient evil being called Fenric.

46 ZYGONS
Shape-changing aliens that crashed into Loch Ness.

47 SUTEKH
Powerful alien that wanted to destroy everything in the universe.

48 NIMON
Parasite creature that looked similar to the Minotaur.

49 SCAROTH
The one-eyed Last of the Jagaroth, who was splintered through time.

50 ZARBI
Large instectoid aliens from the planet Vortis.

ANGEL ATTACK!

HELP THE PONDS GET THROUGH THE MAZE AND BACK TO THE DOCTOR BEFORE THE WEEPING ANGELS ZAP THEM FIFTY YEARS INTO THE PAST!

EXTRA TASK! Try to complete the puzzle without blinking.

START

FINISH

PARLIAMENT HILL, LONDON, JANUARY 1964

WHAT? HOW DID THAT HAPPEN?

LOOK OUT!

LET HER GO!

ARGGH!

STAY AWAY FROM THE SHADOWY CREATURES! THEY'RE HUNGRY FOR SOMETHING.

VREE!

THEY WANT SOMETHING POWERFUL.

NO, THE TARDIS EXISTS IN TWO DIMENSIONS ALREADY AND IS FAR TOO POLITE TO CAUSE THIS MUCH FUSS. THERE'S SOMETHING ELSE. SOMETHING WE'VE *GOT* TO FIND!

THE TARDIS?

MY PHONE. I'VE LOST MY *PHONE*.

THAT'S IT!

GET ON THE SLEDGE NOW. WE'RE GOING TO SAVE YOU! *TRUST ME.*

OF COURSE! A MOBILE PHONE. IN THE WRONG HANDS, ITS *INCREDIBLY* DANGEROUS! THOSE SHADOWS WERE TRYING TO FIND IT. TO THEM IT'S *FOOD*!

SWIPE!

YOU NEED TO GET BEHIND THAT DOOR AND CLOSE IT. AND TAKE YOUR PHONE WITH YOU! YOU'LL BE SAFE ON THE OTHER SIDE!

THANK YOU! BUT WHAT ABOUT THE SHADOWS?

I'VE GOT IT COVERED. NOW GO!

SLAM

SHOULD OUR SHADOW FRIENDS STILL BE HERE?

ER. NO. SO LET'S HOPE THIS WORKS...

VWOORD

VREEEE!

BOOM!

I WONDERED IF WE COULD STAY AND TAKE A LOOK AROUND LONDON IN 1964 FOR A BIT?

WE DID IT! I'M NOT QUITE SURE WHAT WE DID, BUT WE DID IT.

I SENT THE DOOR BACK INTO THE TARDIS. NO MORE TIME CORRIDOR. THE CREATURES COULDN'T EXIST WITHOUT IT. SO BOOM.

DON'T SEE WHY NOT! CARNABY STREET! KING'S ROAD! CAMDEN TOWN! MAYBE LEAVE YOUR MOBILE PHONE IN THE TARDIS THOUGH. JUST IN CASE.

THE END

Nano-cloud DANGER!

THE DALEK NANO-CLOUD IS INTERFERING WITH HOW YOU SEE THESE PICTURES OF OSWIN OSWALD. LOOK AT THEM CLOSELY TO WORK OUT WHICH TWO MATCH EXACTLY.

A

B

C

D

E

F

G

H

Who's Who?

Fifty years of the Doctor!

IT'S HARD TO BELIEVE THAT ONE MAN HAS HAD SO MANY DIFFERENT BODIES. THANKS TO A TIME LORD TRICK CALLED REGENERATION, THE DOCTOR HAS CHANGED HIS APPEARANCE A NUMBER OF TIMES SO FAR...

The First Doctor

(Played by William Hartnell, 1963–66)

The original Doctor was incredibly different from all of his future selves. Quick tempered and often selfish, he didn't like to talk about his home world. One day, after fighting Cybermen, he mentioned his body was 'wearing a bit thin'. He later collapsed in the TARDIS and started to change...

PLUS! 50 YEARS OF COMPANIONS!

The Doctor has had many friends along the way. Here they all are...

Susan Foreman · Ian Chesterton · Barbara Wright · Vicki · Steven Taylor · Katarina · Sara Kingdom · Dodo Chaplet · Ben Jackson · Polly · Jamie McCrimmon

The Second Doctor

(Played by Patrick Troughton, 1966–69)

Although this was the same man, amazingly the Doctor now looked much younger. Gone was his white hair and grumpiness, and in its place was a funny man who liked to joke, play the recorder and disguise himself. His own people, the Time Lords, eventually forced him to regenerate.

The Third Doctor

(Played by Jon Pertwee, 1970–74)

As punishment from the Time Lords for breaking the Laws of Time, the Third Doctor was stranded on Earth without the use of his TARDIS. He became involved with UNIT and helped defend humanity on a regular basis. His body was damaged by radiation and he had to regenerate again.

The Fourth Doctor

(Played by Tom Baker, 1974–81)

Wide-eyed and always full of energy, the Fourth Doctor couldn't wait to get back into the TARDIS and out into time and space after the Third Doctor earned the removal of his exiled status. He loved jelly babies and could charm most people with his smile. He regenerated when he fell from a giant radio telescope while thwarting the Master's plans.

Victoria Waterfield | Zoe Herriot | Liz Shaw | Jo Grant  | Sarah Jane Smith | The Brigadier  | Sergeant Benton | Captain Yates | Harry Sullivan | Leela | K-9 | First Romana | Second Romana

The Fifth Doctor

(Played by Peter Davison, 1981–84)

The youthful Fifth Doctor decided to dress in an Edwardian cricket costume – and once used his cricket skills in space in order to get to his drifting TARDIS! When his body was poisoned on the planet Androzani Minor by raw spectrox, he regenerated again.

The Sixth Doctor

(Played by Colin Baker, 1984–1986)

The poor Sixth Doctor had incredibly bad taste in clothes! He chose to wear bright and brash colours – and these matched his bright and brash character. His regeneration was triggered when the TARDIS crash-landed.

Adric

Nyssa

Tegan Jovanka

Turlough

Kamelion

The Seventh Doctor

(Played by Sylvester McCoy, 1986–1989, 1996)

Always manic, quick thinking and at times, quite manipulative, the Seventh Doctor also had a good sense of humour. Shockingly, he stepped from the TARDIS one day and was shot. He was rushed to hospital and with the doctors confused by his two hearts, left for dead... until eventually another regeneration kicked in.

The Eighth Doctor

(Played by Paul McGann, 1996)

Elegant and looking like a very smart Edwardian gentleman, the Eighth Doctor was possibly the Doctor who got caught up in the Last Great Time War between the Daleks and the Doctor's own people, the Time Lords. We didn't get to see what caused him to regenerate...

Peri Brown

Mel Bush

Ace

Grace Holloway

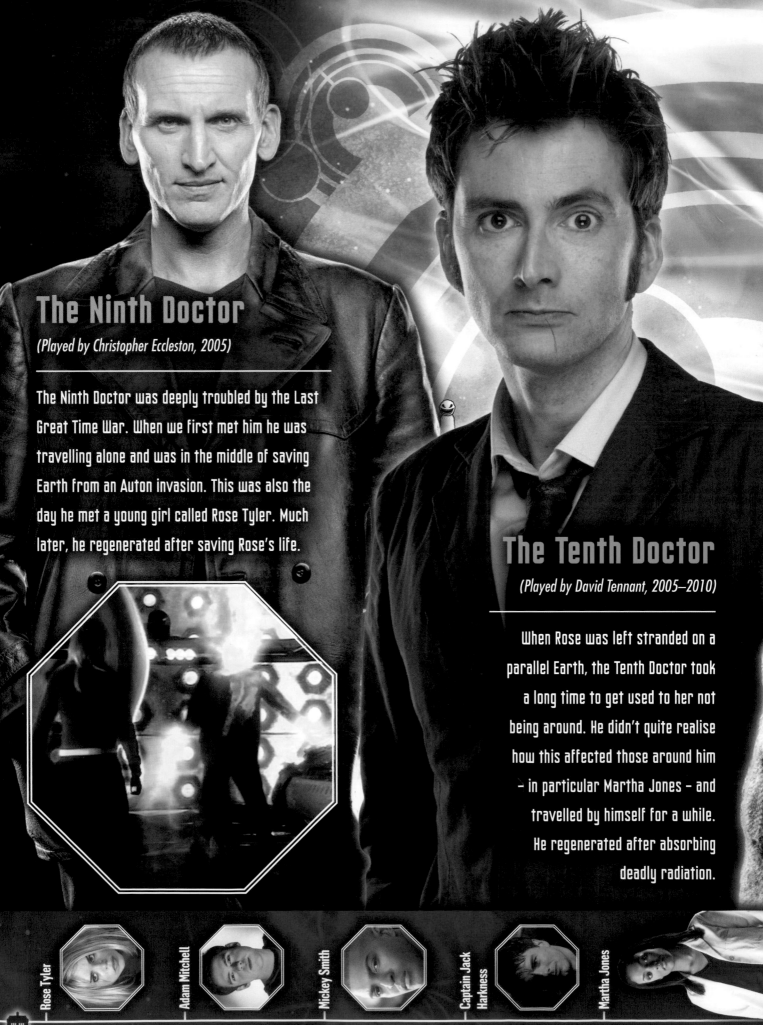

The Ninth Doctor

(Played by Christopher Eccleston, 2005)

The Ninth Doctor was deeply troubled by the Last Great Time War. When we first met him he was travelling alone and was in the middle of saving Earth from an Auton invasion. This was also the day he met a young girl called Rose Tyler. Much later, he regenerated after saving Rose's life.

The Tenth Doctor

(Played by David Tennant, 2005–2010)

When Rose was left stranded on a parallel Earth, the Tenth Doctor took a long time to get used to her not being around. He didn't quite realise how this affected those around him – in particular Martha Jones – and travelled by himself for a while. He regenerated after absorbing deadly radiation.

Rose Tyler

Adam Mitchell

Mickey Smith

Captain Jack Harkness

Martha Jones

The Eleventh Doctor

(Played by Matt Smith, 2010–present)

And here's the current Doctor – the youngest looking Doctor so far. This Doctor loves hats – including a fez and a Stetson! He also wears bow ties, because, as he says, bow ties are cool.

Donna Noble

Wilfred Mott

Amy Pond

Rory Williams

River Song

Clara Oswald

That Impossible Girl

This is Clara – the girl the Doctor keeps meeting throughout time!

Who is she?

The Doctor is very confused by his friend, Clara Oswald, because versions of the brave girl appeared in several different places in time as well as space. It took a while until the reason was finally revealed...

Oswin Oswald

Long before Clara joined the Doctor, a girl called Oswin Oswald helped the Doctor defeat the Daleks. The junior entertainment manager on the *Starship Alaska* had been converted into a Dalek herself, but had blanked out the horrible truth. Before she died, her last words were: 'Run, you clever boy... and remember...'

Victorian Clara

This version of Clara worked as a barmaid but had a secret life looking after two children. Clara helped the Doctor fight alien snow and vicious snowmen but was killed after falling from a great height. Her dying words were the same as Oswin's...

Clara Oswald

Desperate to find out who this girl actually is, the Doctor heads to present-day Earth and meets another Clara. This Clara helps him defeat the Great Intelligence again and accepts the Doctor's offer to travel with him. The Doctor still wants to know who she is!

Travelling in the TARDIS

The Doctor and Clara had the best adventures together, meeting so many different monsters, travelling to so many amazing worlds. The TARDIS sensed there was something unusual about Clara — and she felt that it didn't like her. Clara called the TARDIS a grumpy old cow!

Saving the Doctor

Finally, to save the Doctor and the universe from damage caused by the Great Intelligence at Trenzalore, Clara stepped into a time rift and was torn apart by time winds. Millions of different versions of Clara suddenly existed in time and space… but the Doctor was determined to get her back.

DID YOU KNOW?

Clara becomes a computer expert when she is downloaded from the Great Intelligence's Data Cloud.

THE FIFTY-YEAR DELAY

Ryan Goodman was running late for work again.

On a cold November morning, he rushed into the Underground station, dashed through the ticket barrier and down onto a slow-moving escalator that lead to the southbound platform of the Northern Line.

When he arrived on the platform – hot and out of breath – he realised he was the only person waiting for a train. It was eerily quiet. Ryan looked up at the display that tells you how long you have to wait.

Kennington via Charing Cross – 50 years.

Very funny, he thought, as he stared into the dark tunnel at the end of the platform.

Suddenly, there was a blast of air from nowhere. It blew a discarded newspaper onto the tracks. Ryan presumed it was the train. But although there was a noise of *something* and a draught from *somewhere*, no train appeared.

Instead, a large blue box with windows on each side and a flashing light on top faded noisily into existence in the middle of the platform. Ryan stared open-mouthed at the blue box as everything went quiet and the light stopped flashing.

A door flew inwards, and a man in a bow tie and smart jacket came thundering out.

'Stay behind the yellow line,' he shouted.

He didn't look like he worked for London Underground but, nevertheless, he had an air of authority about him. Ryan obediently stayed behind the yellow line painted on the edge of the platform.

'How did you do that?' asked Ryan. 'You know, with your box? Do you work for the police?'

'The short answer is no.'

Ryan stared at the man.

'So… what about the long answer?'

A roaring sound came from somewhere in the southbound tunnel. It didn't sound like a train.

'An ancient time bird is a bit lost and I'm trying to help her! She's causing all sorts of naughtiness and time disruptions. We're actually fifty years in your future.'

'Really? I mean… *what?*'

The roaring sound was getting louder.

'Yes, really. And we can sort it. Are you ready?' said the man.

Before he could answer, Ryan watched as a huge brightly-coloured bird flew out of the tunnel. It shimmered and looked as if it was on fire. The creature seemed to fade in and out of existence as it looped over their heads and up and down the tracks. It was beautiful.

And then there was another sound. One that Ryan heard almost daily. The sound of a tube train thundering through tunnels…

'There's a train coming!' cried Ryan.

'It's okay – she's spotted the TARDIS.'

Time slowed down. A tube train appeared at the mouth of the tunnel and Ryan watched as the bird flew out of its way, missing it by a split second. He tried to shout at the man… but words wouldn't come out of his mouth quickly enough. In slow motion, the strange man and Ryan ran towards the bird.

The bird turned sharply and started flying towards the two men. It flew over their heads and through one of the doors of the blue box.

The ground started shaking as time sped up again.

'Everything's resetting. She knows she's safe now.'

Ryan watched as the tube train

disappeared before it reached the end of the platform. The ground stopped shaking and suddenly the platform was filled with people. None of them took any interest in the large blue box or the man standing next to it.

Ryan looked up at the board.

Kennington via Charing Cross – 1 min.

'Everything's back to normal thanks to us. Slight delay on the Central line, but what's new?' said the man from the box.

'But, what just happened?'

'We just saved an ancient time bird. I'd better get her home though… thank you for your help.'

A tube train rumbled out of the tunnel. Ryan watched as the man went back inside the blue box and shut the door. As people on the platform pushed onto the train, only Ryan noticed as the light on top of the box starting flashing and it slowly disappeared…

There are a massive 50 differences to spot in these two pictures.

CAN YOU FIND THEM ALL?

The Great Intelligence

A powerful enemy of the Doctor's, the Intelligence is extremely dangerous. Whatever you do, don't let it get inside your head.

What is it?

The Great Intelligence was created from a lonely child's darkest thoughts and since then has wanted to take human form. Because it doesn't have a proper physical form it must possess people instead.

Dr Simeon

Walter Simeon was the lonely child. He was outside building a snowman when he heard a strange voice talking to him. Since that day, the Great Intelligence controlled Walter's body. It waited until the time was right for an invasion of Earth with dangerous alien snow.

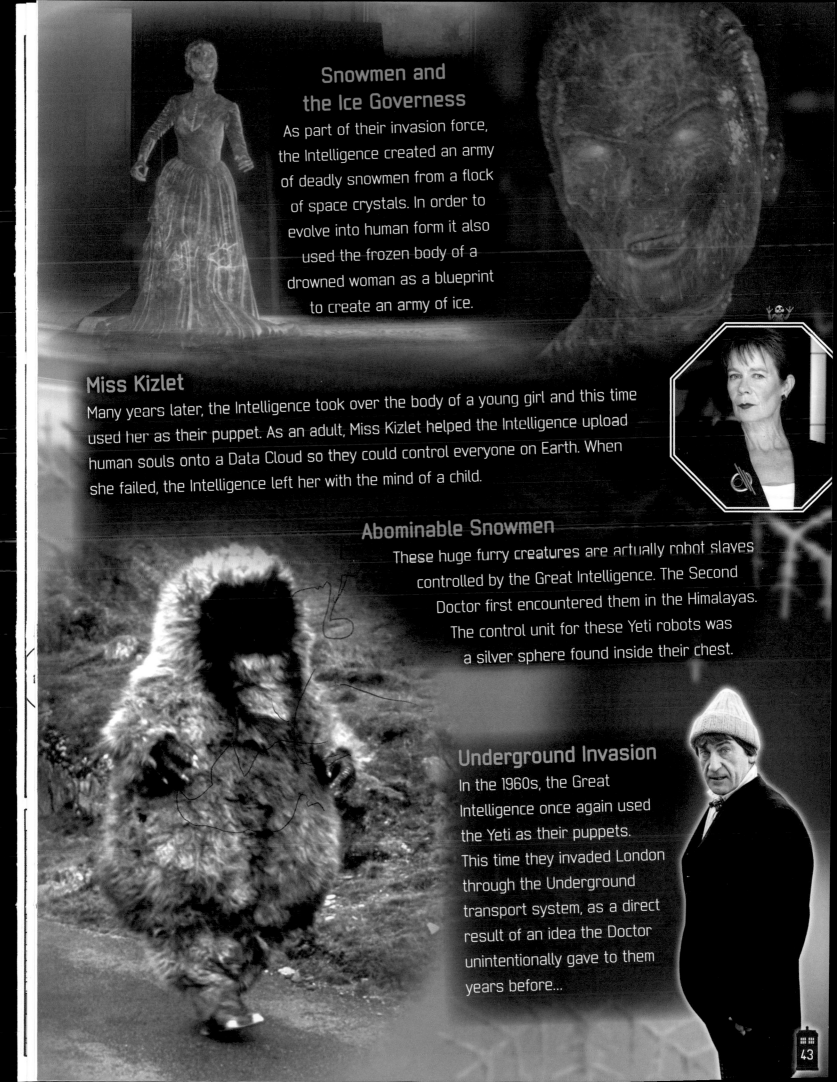

Snowmen and the Ice Governess

As part of their invasion force, the Intelligence created an army of deadly snowmen from a flock of space crystals. In order to evolve into human form it also used the frozen body of a drowned woman as a blueprint to create an army of ice.

Miss Kizlet

Many years later, the Intelligence took over the body of a young girl and this time used her as their puppet. As an adult, Miss Kizlet helped the Intelligence upload human souls onto a Data Cloud so they could control everyone on Earth. When she failed, the Intelligence left her with the mind of a child.

Abominable Snowmen

These huge furry creatures are actually robot slaves controlled by the Great Intelligence. The Second Doctor first encountered them in the Himalayas. The control unit for these Yeti robots was a silver sphere found inside their chest.

Underground Invasion

In the 1960s, the Great Intelligence once again used the Yeti as their puppets. This time they invaded London through the Underground transport system, as a direct result of an idea the Doctor unintentionally gave to them years before...

The Ice Warriors

Meet the proud race from planet Mars!

Warriors from Mars

The Ice Warriors are from the planet Mars – and the Doctor knows all about them as he has met them several times. They are a race of large, noble reptilian humanoids that can withstand extremely cold temperatures.

Survival

The warriors are bio-mechanoid cyborgs. When Mars turned cold the creatures had to adapt. They built themselves survival armour so they could exist in the freezing cold temperatures of their homeworld. Their massive armoured bodies have sonic weapons built-in to one of their arms.

Strengths and Weaknesses

The tough armour protects the smaller Martian creature inside. Bullets won't harm the warrior, but electricity and heat will. Turn up the heat, and the Martian warrior will find it difficult to breathe and will eventually die.

Inside the suit

Ice Warriors find it dishonourable to leave their suit – and will only get out of it in extreme circumstances. Inside the bulky suit is a scaly green creature that can move incredibly quickly. It has huge liquid-black eyes, a cracked tortoise-like mouth, and incredibly powerful claws.

Hero

Grand Marshal Skaldak was the greatest hero the Martian race ever produced. He was frozen in the Arctic ice for 5000 years and when he defrosted inside a submarine en route to Moscow, he went on the rampage.

The Second Ice Age

The Doctor first encountered the Ice Warriors during the Second Ice Age on Earth, when a warrior and its spaceship were found in a glacier. With Mars now dead, the Ice Warrior started to revive its race, with plans to make Earth its new home.

The Cybermen

TALL, STRONG, EMOTIONLESS AND MADE OF STEEL – MEET THE ULTIMATE UPGRADE...

IN THE BEGINNING

Cybermen are one of the most dangerous and powerful races in the universe. Years ago, on Earth's twin planet Mondas, humans replaced parts of their bodies with artificial ones and horrific cloth-faced Cybermen (still with human hands) were created.

PARALLEL EARTH

Similarly, on a parallel Earth, where things are slightly different from our own Earth, John Lumic had the same idea and created a master race of upgraded humans. These silver giants had factories all around the world and had one single intention – to upgrade everyone to be like them.

ESSENTIAL UPGRADES!

The Doctor has met the Cybermen many times throughout his long life. He has watched the Cybermen grow stronger and stronger and change their appearance several times (although not as many times as he has changed his).

ARMY OF GHOSTS

Lumic's Cybermen came through into our Earth when a Void ship containing millions of Daleks broke down the barrier between worlds. The Cybermen suggested working together with the Daleks but the Daleks refused – and this started a huge battle between the two races.

After a long hard war, it was thought that the Cybermen were extinct for over a thousand years. What people didn't realise was that while the battle raged between humans and the Cyberiad, the Cybermen were repairing Cyber units one by one to create undefeatable versions.

DID YOU KNOW?

Early versions of Cybermen were allergic to gold.

THE ARMY AWAKES!

When the time was right – and the most perfect version of the Cybermen was ready – massive armies of new-improved Cybermen pushed their way out of Cyber bunkers ready to take on the universe. Luckily, the Doctor and Clara helped destroy them all... we hope.

The BIG Quiz!

Get ready to strain your brain with this amazing quiz! Can you answer these fifty questions about *Doctor Who*?

TOP TIP! You'll find all the answers in this book!

1. What year did *Doctor Who* first appear on television?

   1963

2. What is the name of the Doctor's granddaughter?

   Susan Foreman

3. What words appear between POLICE BOX on the Doctor's TARDIS?

   Public Call

4. What was Grand Marshal Skaldak?

   Ice Warrior

5. True or false? The TARDIS should be able to change its appearance wherever it goes.

   true

6. Where were TARDISes grown?

   On Gallifrey.

7. What does the R stand for in TARDIS?

   Relative

8. How many hearts does the Doctor have?

   2

9. Who is the Doctor married to?

   River Song

10. What creatures will move if you blink?

    Weeping Angel

11. What family comes from Raxacoricofallapatorius?

    Slitheen

12. Who is this?

    K9

54

13. What is the name of the junior entertainment manager on the *Starship Alaska*? ~~Oswin~~ Oswald

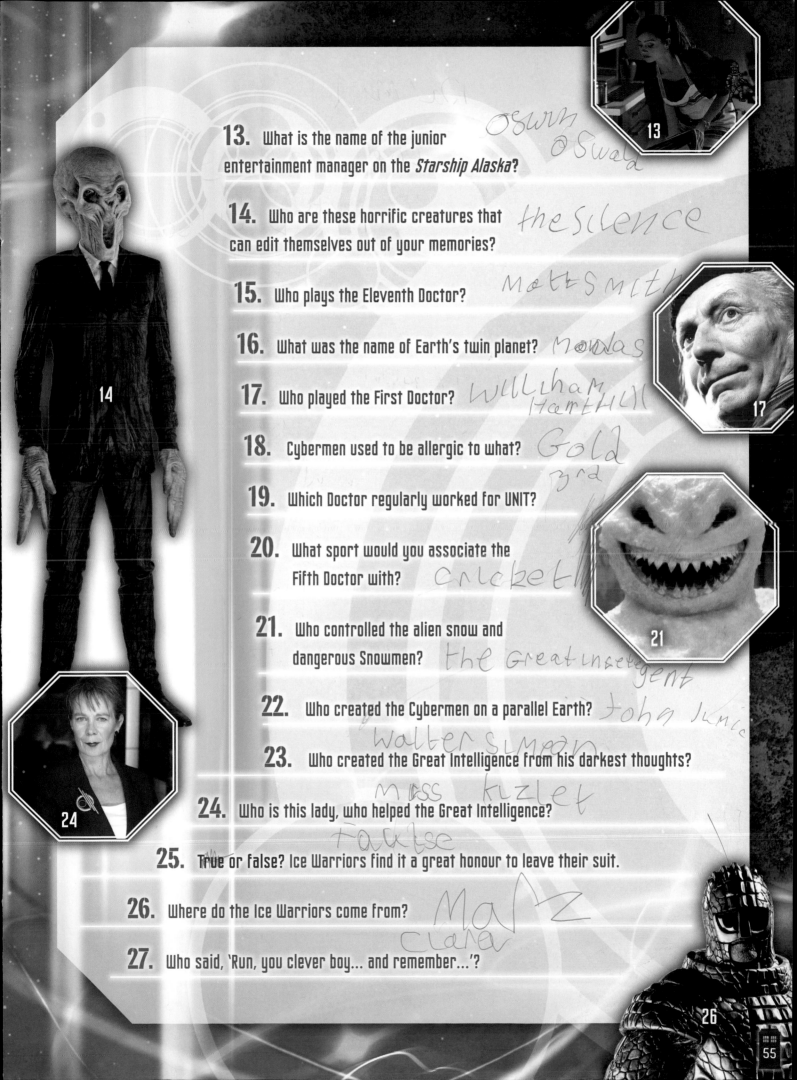
13

14. Who are these horrific creatures that can edit themselves out of your memories? the silence

14

15. Who plays the Eleventh Doctor? Matt Smith

16. What was the name of Earth's twin planet? Mondas

17. Who played the First Doctor? William Hartnell

17

18. Cybermen used to be allergic to what? Gold

19. Which Doctor regularly worked for UNIT? 3rd

20. What sport would you associate the Fifth Doctor with? cricket

21

21. Who controlled the alien snow and dangerous Snowmen? the Great Intelligent

22. Who created the Cybermen on a parallel Earth? John Lumic

23. Who created the Great Intelligence from his darkest thoughts? Walter Simeon

24. Who is this lady, who helped the Great Intelligence? Miss Kizlet

24

25. ~~True~~ or false? Ice Warriors find it a great honour to leave their suit. False

26. Where do the Ice Warriors come from? Mars

27. Who said, 'Run, you clever boy... and remember...'? Clara

26

55

28. Clara looked after Victorian children. What else did she do?

barmaid

29. Who does Clara think is a grumpy old cow?

the TaRDIS

30. Who played the Fifth Doctor?

Peter Davidson

31. What was the Doctor's nickname when he was younger?

theta sigma

32. Who wiped the Daleks' memory of the Doctor?

oswin

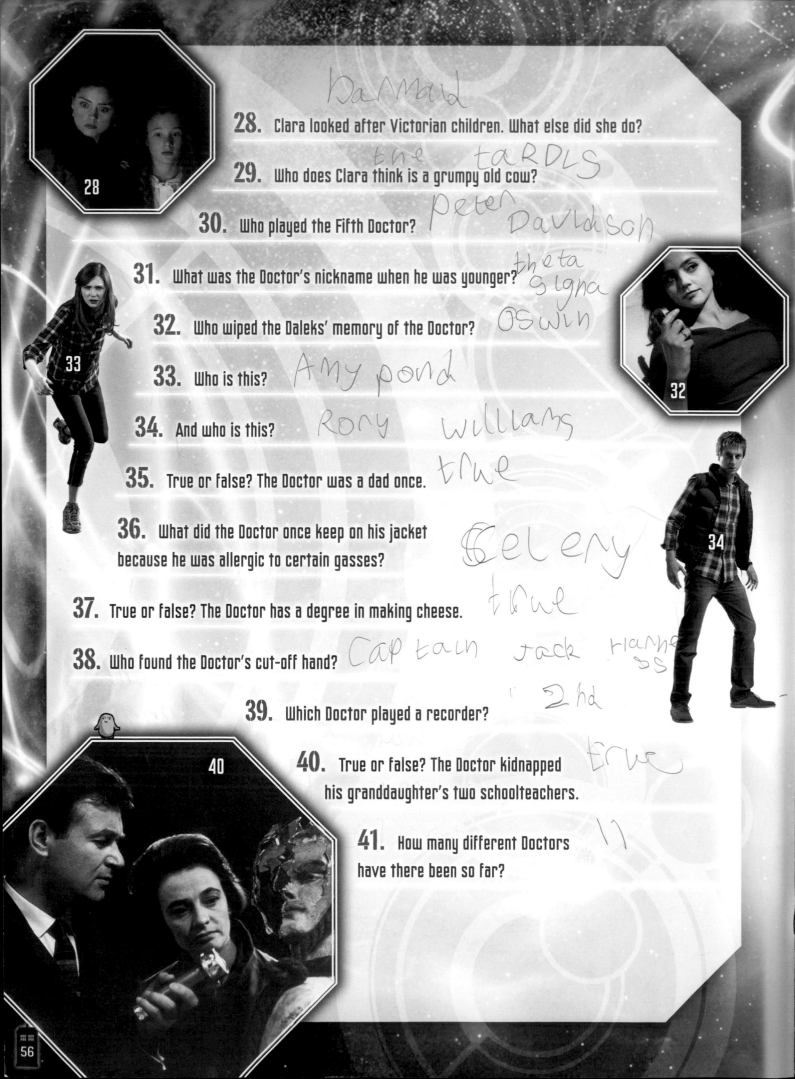

33. Who is this?

Amy pond

34. And who is this?

Rory williams

35. True or false? The Doctor was a dad once.

true

36. What did the Doctor once keep on his jacket because he was allergic to certain gasses?

celery

37. True or false? The Doctor has a degree in making cheese.

true

38. Who found the Doctor's cut-off hand?

captain Jack Harkness

39. Which Doctor played a recorder?

2nd

40. True or false? The Doctor kidnapped his granddaughter's two schoolteachers.

true

41. How many different Doctors have there been so far?

11

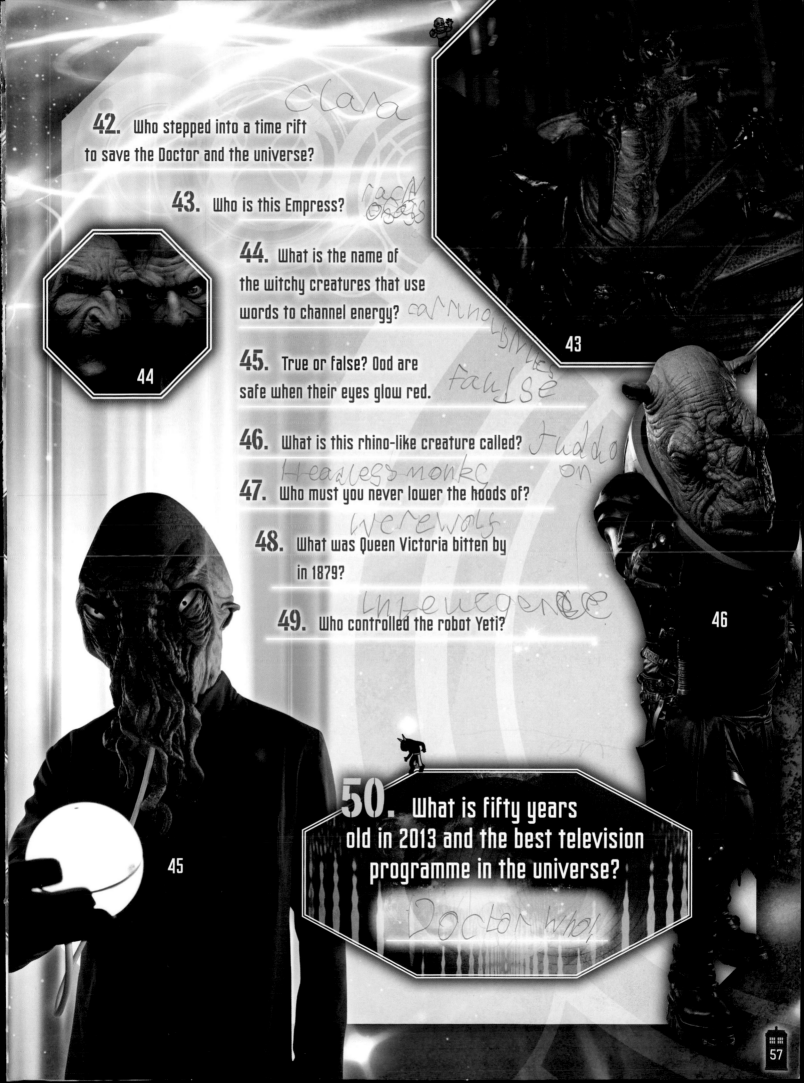

42. Who stepped into a time rift to save the Doctor and the universe?

Clara

43. Who is this Empress? *racN ofass*

44. What is the name of the witchy creatures that use words to channel energy? *carmnousmes*

44

43

45. True or false? Ood are safe when their eyes glow red. *faulse*

46. What is this rhino-like creature called? *Juddo on*

47. Who must you never lower the hoods of? *Headless monks*

48. What was Queen Victoria bitten by in 1879? *werewols*

49. Who controlled the robot Yeti? *Intelegence*

46

45

50. What is fifty years old in 2013 and the best television programme in the universe?

Doctor who

ANSWERS

Angel Attack! – *page 22*

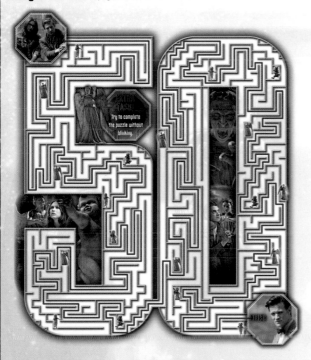

Nano-cloud Danger – *page 29*
Clara B and H match

Spot the Difference – *pages 40-41*

ANSWERS

The BIG Quiz – *pages 54-57*

1. 1963
2. Susan Foreman
3. Public Call
4. An Ice Warrior
5. True
6. Gallifrey
7. Relative
8. Two
9. River Song
10. The Weeping Angels
11. Slitheen
12. K-9
13. Oswin Oswald
14. The Silence
15. Matt Smith
16. Mondas
17. William Hartnell
18. Gold
19. The Third Doctor
20. Cricket
21. The Great Intelligence
22. John Lumic
23. Walter Simeon
24. Miss Kizlet
25. False
26. Mars
27. Oswin/Clara
28. She was a barmaid
29. The TARDIS!
30. Peter Davison
31. Theta Sigma
32. Oswin Oswald
33. Amy Pond/Williams
34. Rory Williams
35. True
36. Celery
37. True
38. Captain Jack Harkness
39. The Second Doctor
40. True
41. Eleven
42. Clara Oswald
43. Empress of the Racnoss
44. Carrionites
45. False
46. Judoon
47. The Headless Monks
48. A werewolf
49. The Great Intelligence
50. *Doctor Who!*